1,00

HENRY

D1061662

JAMES

PERCY

MEET ALL THESE FRIENDS IN BUZZ BOOKS:

Thomas the Tank Engine
The Animals of Farthing Wood
Biker Mice From Mars
James Bond Junior
Fireman Sam
Joshua Jones
Rupert
Babar

First published in Great Britain 1992
by Buzz Books, an imprint of Reed Children's Books
Michelin House, 81 Fulham Road, London SW3 6RB
and Auckland, Melbourne, Singapore and Toronto

Reprinted 1993 (twice)

Copyright © William Heinemann Limited 1992

All publishing rights: William Heinemann Limited.
All television and merchandising rights licensed by
William Heinemann Limited to Britt Allcroft (Thomas) Limited
exclusively, worldwide.

Photographs © Britt Allcroft (Thomas) Limited 1992
Photographs by David Mitton and Terry Permane
for Britt Allcroft's production of Thomas the Tank
Engine and Friends

ISBN 1 85591 223 6

Printed in Italy by LEGO

THOMAS GETS BUMPED

buzz books

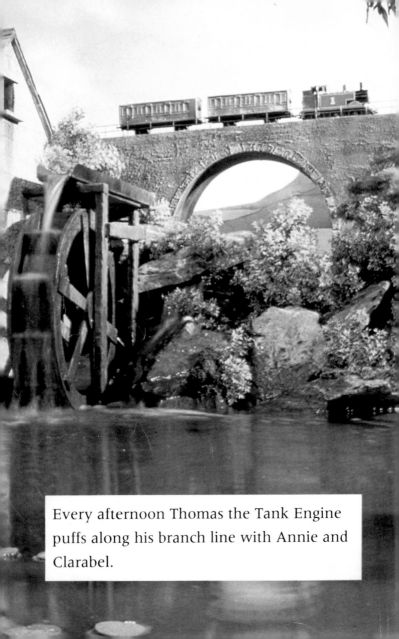

Every afternoon Thomas the Tank Engine puffs along his branch line with Annie and Clarabel.

First they pass the water mill. Next they come to a big farm.

Then, they can see a bridge with a village nestled either side of it.
This is a special place.

Whenever children hear Thomas coming along, they stand on the bridge waving until he is out of sight.

One day Thomas was running late. He had stopped at the signal before the bridge to talk to some new children.

Percy was waiting too.

"Hurry up Thomas," called Percy when the signal dropped. "If you're late the Fat Controller may get a new engine to replace you."

"He would never do that," thought Thomas. But he was worried.

Next day, Thomas hurried along the line. Just ahead was the goods yard. There, on the platform, was an inspector waving a red flag.

Next Thomas saw some children. They were waving too.

"Something must be wrong," thought Thomas. "This station is for goods not passengers."

"Help Thomas, help. We are glad to see you," called the children. "Please will you take us home?"

The station master explained to Thomas's driver that the school bus had broken down and all the parents would be worried if the children were late.

13

Thomas waited as the children walked down from the bridge. Then he took them to the next station where Bertie was waiting to take them home.

When Thomas finished his journey he was very late. He was worried that the Fat Controller might be cross with him.

"I warned Thomas," puffed Percy to James. "He's been late one time too many. He'll be in trouble now."

But next morning the Fat Controller was nowhere to be seen.

"Thank goodness," sighed Thomas.

Thomas knows every part of his branch line, but just ahead was a stretch where the hot sun had bent the rails on the track.

"Careful Thomas," called his driver. But it was too late.

"That's done it," said his driver. "We shan't get any further today."

"But what about my passengers?"

"Don't worry. They'll be looked after," replied his driver.

While workmen repaired the line, Thomas had to shunt trucks in the yard.

Bertie came to see him.

"I understand you need my help again."

"Yes Bertie," replied Thomas sadly. "I can't run without my rails."

Bertie set off to collect Thomas's passengers.

"Hello Bertie," they said. "We are glad you are here."

Bertie drove along the road that runs by the railway. He stopped at each station along the line. Sometimes he stopped between stations to let people off closer to their homes.

Thomas felt miserable.

"I've lost my passengers. They'll like Bertie better than me."

The Fat Controller arrived.

"Your branch line is repaired. I'm going to change your timetable so that you and Bertie can work together more."

When Thomas reached the station, there were all his passengers.

"Bertie is a good bus, but we missed our train rides with you," they said.

Later Thomas spoke to Bertie.

"Thank you for looking after my passengers."

"That's alright, Thomas. I like to make new friends, but I'm glad to share them with you."

"Bertie," said Thomas, "you're a good friend indeed."

THOMAS

EDWARD

GORDON